The Spade Sage

The Spade Sage

A Jataka Tale

Illustrated by Sherri Nestorowich

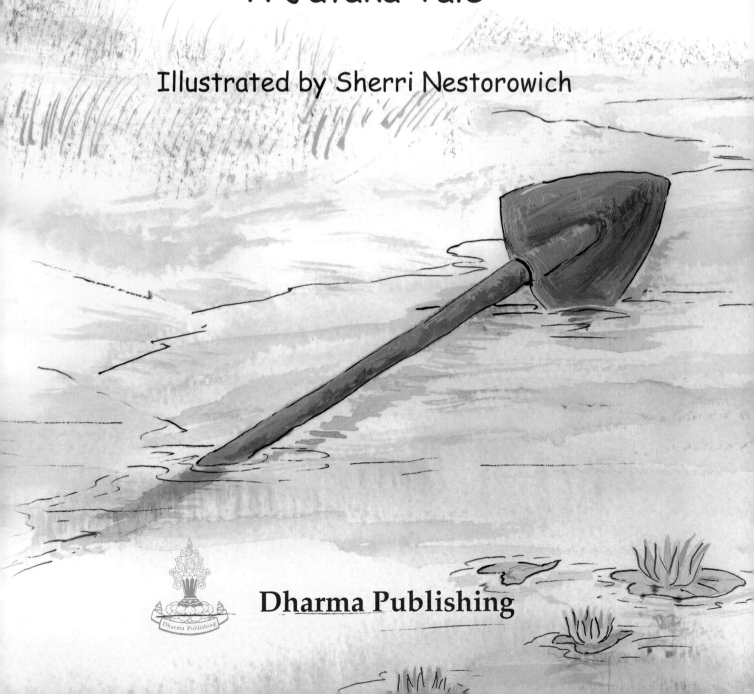

Dharma Publishing

Jataka Tales Series

Story adapted by Dharma Publishing editorial staff
Illustrated by Sherri Nestorowich
Printed in the USA by Dharma Press
2910 San Pablo Avenue, Berkeley, California 94702

Library of Congress Cataloging-in-Publication Data

The Spade Sage : a Jataka tale / illustrated by Sherri Nestorowich.
p. cm. — (Jataka tales series)
Summary: His attachment to a humble spade shows a poor gardener
the way to conquer his desires and achieve happiness.
ISBN 0–89800–321–0 (pbk.)
1. Jataka stories, English. 2. Gautama Buddha
—Pre-existence—Juvenile literature. [1. Jataka stories.]
I. Nestorowich, Sherri, 1967 - ill. II. Tipitaka. Suttapitaka.
Khuddakanikaya. Jataka. III. Series.
BQ1462.E5 S63 2002   294.3'82325--dc21   2002031570

Dedicated to
children
everywhere

The Jataka Tales

The Jataka Tales celebrate the power of action motivated by compassion, love, wisdom, and kindness. They teach that all we think and do profoundly affects the quality of our lives. Selfish words and deeds bring suffering to us and to those around us while selfless action gives rise to goodness of such power that it spreads in ever-widening circles, uplifting all forms of life.

The Jataka Tales, first related by the Buddha over two thousand years ago, bring to light his many lifetimes of positive action practiced for the sake of the world. As an embodiment of great compassion, the Awakened One reappears in many forms and in many times and places to ease the suffering of living beings. Thus these stories are filled with heroes of all kinds, each demonstrating the power of compassion and wisdom to transform any situation.

While based on traditional accounts, the stories in the Jataka Tales Series have been adapted for the children of today. May these tales inspire the positive action that will sustain the heart of goodness and the light of wisdom for the future of the world.

Tarthang Tulku   Founder, Dharma Publishing

Once upon a time, near a great city in India, the Buddha was born as a gardener called the Spade Sage. He was called this because everywhere he went he carried his only possession, a garden spade.

Using only this spade, he earned a living growing great orange pumpkins, shiny cucumbers, ruby red radishes, crisp lettuces, and many other vegetables on a small patch of ground.

One day the Spade Sage thought to himself, "Though my garden is a good one and my vegetables are the best, I am not happy. I must give up my spade and go into the forest to become a hermit. I must try to discover the secret of happiness which is locked within my own mind."

So, leaving his spade and his garden behind,
he set out for the forest.

However, when the Spade Sage got to the forest, he found he was restless and longed for his old life. He wanted to return to his one spade and his little garden.

He thought and dreamed about these things so often that he finally admitted to himself, "This idea of mine to come into the forest, away from all other men, was a foolish one. I can only think of my old home and my old habits. I will never find the secret of happiness this way."

What an unfortunate gardener! Soon after he returned to his digging and weeding, he began to see that he had been wrong to leave the forest and come back to the world of men. For he was still not happy. He thought, "I was only greedy for my life and my comforts. For the sake of one spade and a few vegetables, I have given up my chance to find the secret of happiness which is locked within my own mind. Tomorrow I will return to the forest and again become a hermit.

But even the Spade Sage himself did not know how great his desire was for the world of men. Even after he had gone to the forest for a second time, his spade and his garden called him back to his old life. Indeed, a full seven times he had left his garden and then returned to it again.

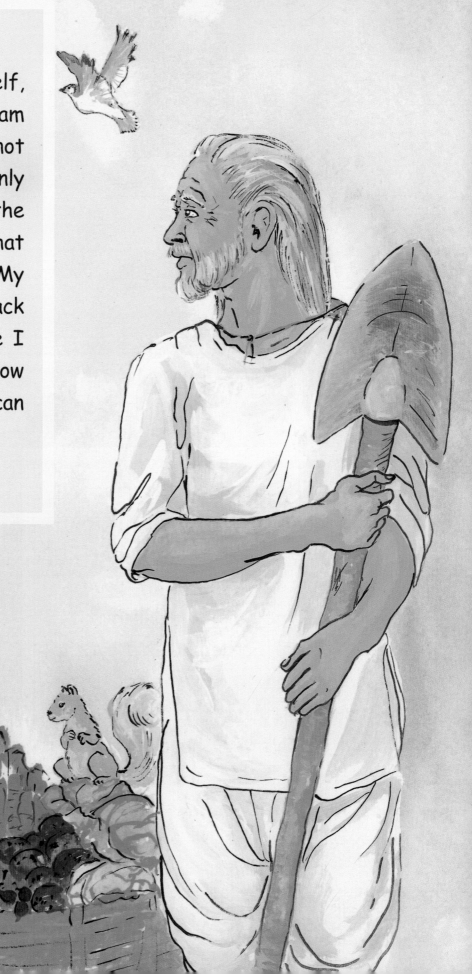

At last he said to himself, "This is foolishness. I am a poor man. Yet, I cannot give up my one and only possession to find the secret of happiness that is within my own mind. My spade keeps calling me back to everyday life. Before I leave this time I will throw it into the river where I can never find it again."

Carrying his spade, the Spade Sage went to the edge of the river. There again he thought, "I must not look where my spade falls or I may wish to fish it out again later." So he shut his eyes, spun around three times, and threw his spade into the river. Then he felt very happy, for he had finally overcome his desire. He had thrown away his spade once and for all.

Filled with joy, he began to shout in a loud and deep voice that echoed through the hills like the roar of a lion:

"I have conquered!

I have conquered!"

ow just at that moment, a great king was riding by on a splendid elephant. He had just protected his kingdom by winning a very important battle, and he was now on his way home.

When the king heard the Spade Sage shouting, he said to one of his servants, "Here is a man shouting that he has conquered! I wonder whom he has conquered? Bring him to me so that I may find out."

And so the Spade Sage came before the king, and the king said to him, "Sir, you say that you have conquered. I myself am a conqueror. I have just won a great battle and am on my way home. But whom have you conquered?"

"Good King," said the Spade Sage, "a thousand of your victories are nothing compared to my victory. You have only conquered other men. I have conquered my own desire by throwing my spade into the river."

In that instant, the Spade Sage looked within his mind. Freed from attachment to his spade, he found the secret of happiness and became a very wise man. Then, as the king and his people looked in wonder, the Spade Sage rose into the air, calling them to follow him. As they listened to the words of the Spade Sage, they too learned how to conquer their desires and find the secret of happiness within their minds.

And so it happened that a poor gardener named the Spade Sage became a wise man and a great teacher.

After telling this story, the Buddha said, "A long time ago, the good and wise tried seven times before they could finally overcome their desire and find the secret of happiness locked in their own minds. Ananda, you were the king of those days, and I was the Spade Sage."

The Jataka Tales Series

Golden Foot
Heart of Gold
Pieces of Gold
The Spade Sage
A Precious Life
Three Wise Birds
The Best of Friends
Courageous Captain
The Hunter and the Quail
The Parrot and the Fig Tree
The Proud Peacock and the Mallard
The King Who Understood Animals
Great Gift and the Wish-Fulfilling Gem
Wisdom of the Golden Goose
The Monkey King
The Value of Friends
The Magic of Patience
The Power of a Promise
The Rabbit in the Moon
The Jewel of Friendship
The Fish King's Power of Truth
The Rabbit Who Overcame Fear
A Wise Ape Teaches Kindness
The Princess Who Overcame Evil